HAPPY BIRTHDAY, PRINCESS

For my daughter Heidi and other real life princesses – M. R.

For Moomy, who never made me wear pink – V. G.

First published in hardback and paperback in Great Britain by HarperCollins *Children's Books* in 2019

1 3 5 7 9 10 8 6 4 2

HB ISBN: 978-0-00-824962-5
PB ISBN: 978-0-00-822716-6

HarperCollins *Children's Books* is a division of HarperCollins *Publishers* Ltd.

Text and illustrations copyright © HarperCollins *Publishers* Ltd 2019

Visit our website at: www.harpercollins.co.uk

Printed in China

MIX
Paper from
responsible sources
FSC™ C007454

This book is produced from independently certified FSC™ paper
to ensure responsible forest management.

For more information visit: www.harpercollins.co.uk/green

Happy Birthday to you, Princess

written by
Michelle Robinson

illustrated by
Vicki Gausden

HarperCollins *Children's Books*

Happy birthday to you!

Happy birthday to you!

Happy birthday, dear Princess.

May your wishes come true!

Time to go for a spin . . .

Trumpets welcome you in.

Wishes granted ...

you're enchanted ...

Let the **party** begin!

There's a **troll** in your sled.

There's a pea in your bed!

A prince wants to kiss you ...

But a frog does **instead!**

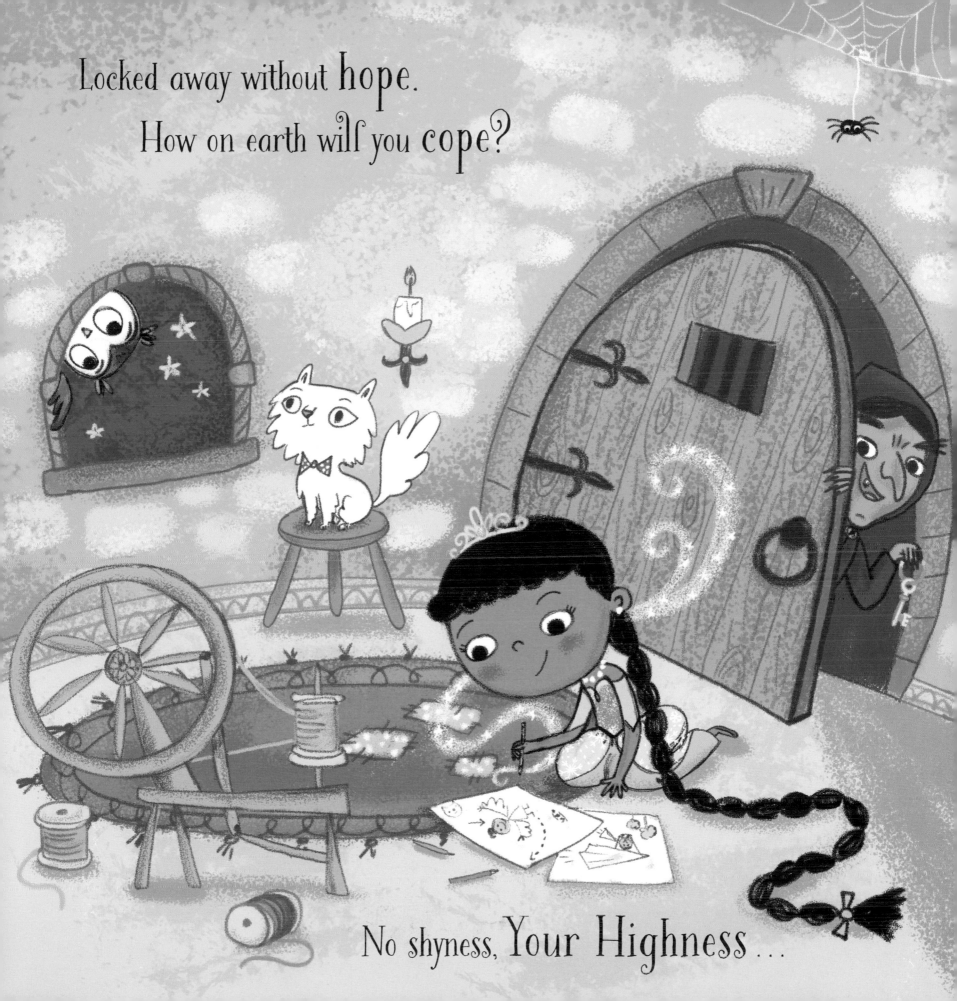

Locked away without hope.
How on earth will you cope?

No shyness, Your Highness . . .

Use your hair as a rope!

Clock says one minute to ...
Hope you don't lose a shoe.

Your carriage is a pumpkin
and your driver's a shrew!

You can come back and stay

where the unicorns play...

Happy birthday, dear Princess!

This is your special day.

Turn the page for a Princess activity...

MAKE A PRINCESS CROWN

Play Princess with your very own crown!

YOU WILL NEED:

★ A stapler with staples

★ Cardboard

★ Elastic or ribbon - make a loop big enough to fit around your head

★ Crown decorations - coloured pencils and pens, glitter, stick-on jewels

How to Make Your Crown

1. Trace the crown template onto a piece of cardboard, and cut it out.

2. Decorate your crown! You can colour it in, or cover it in glitter and jewels... How sparkly can you make yours?

3. When your crown is decorated and any glue has dried, use the stapler to secure it to the elastic or ribbon that fits around your head.

Ask a grown-up for help using scissors!

TEMPLATE TO DRAW AROUND

ATTATCH RIBBON OR ELASTIC ON CROSSES

Put on your crown, and greet your subjects!

Bye Bye!